THE BIGGEST SOAP

Carole Lexa Schaefer

Pictures by Stacey Dressen-McQueen

Melanie Kroupa Books   Farrar, Straus and Giroux   New York

Text copyright © 2004 by Carole Lexa Schaefer
Illustrations copyright © 2004 by Stacey Dressen-McQueen
All rights reserved
Distributed in Canada by Douglas & McIntyre Ltd.
Color separations by Chroma Graphics PTE Ltd.
Printed and bound in the United States of America
by Berryville Graphics
Designed by Jennifer Crilly and Barbara Grzeslo
First edition, 2004
10 9 8 7 6 5 4 3 2 1

www.fsgkidsbooks.com

Library of Congress Cataloging-in-Publication Data
Schaefer, Carole Lexa.
    The biggest soap / by Carole Lexa Schaefer ; pictures
by Stacey Dressen-McQueen.— 1st ed.
       p.   cm.
    Summary: When Kessy, who lives in the Truk Islands,
is sent by his mother to buy laundry soap, he hurries
back to listen to her storytelling, discovering that his own
experience makes a good story too.
    ISBN 0-374-30690-7
    [1. Soap—Fiction.   2. Storytelling—Fiction.   3. Chuuk
(Micronesia)—Fiction.   4. Micronesia (Federated States)
—Fiction.]   I. Dressen-McQueen, Stacey, ill.   II. Title.

PZ7.S3315Bi 2004
[E]—dc21
                                    2003048512

In tribute to all the generous Truk islanders,
and to the indomitable spirit of Howard Seay.
With special thanks to Mark and Judy Pederson,
Jack and Anne Weiss, and George Zander.
—C.L.S.

To Rob and Finn with love
—S.D.M.

One morning, Mama hollered to her cousins up the hill, "Ooo-hoo! Let's do laundry today."

"Ooo-hoo," her cousins called back. "Okay."

"Hooray!" cheered Kessy. On laundry days, he got to jump into the sun-warmed washing pool and listen to Mama and her cousins tell stories.

When I'm big enough, thought Kessy, I'll tell stories, too.

"Uh-oh, I'm almost out of soap," said Mama. "Go to the store, my little Kessy, and bring back the biggest piece of laundry soap on Minda's shelf."

Kessy frowned. He was proud that Mama picked him to go to Minda's Store. But he didn't want to miss a single story at the washing pool.

"To get back in time," he told himself, "I'll have to be fast as a typhoon wind."

But no sooner had Kessy reached the mangrove trees along the way when two mud-covered creatures popped out of the water.

"Grrr!" growled one.

"Come clos-s-ser," hissed the other.

"You don't scare me," Kessy told his two older brothers.

"Then play Sea Monsters with us, little boy," said Timus.

"You can be Itty-Bitty Baby Crab," said Berto. "Just like always."

Kessy stepped toward the mud. He'd show them he was bigger than a baby. Then he stopped. "Wait, I can't play," he cried. "I have to buy the biggest soap for Mama." And away he raced.

Above the path, Uncle Cho called, "Halloo, little Kessy. I'm making a new bamboo window for my house. Come and see."

Kessy paused. Cho was his favorite uncle and the best builder on the island. He always let Kessy help. But Kessy called back, "Sorry, Uncle, I've got to buy the biggest soap for Mama—*fast*."

Near the beach, Kessy spied his friend Amina sitting on a driftwood log. She looked at him through a tin can with holes poked in one end. "Want to look through my camera?" she asked.

What would the long path look like through Amina's camera, Kessy wondered. He slowed down. "I'd like to look," he said, "but I've got to get the biggest soap for Mama—right now!"

At Minda's Store, between cans of mackerel and boxes of matches, Kessy spied a stack of soap. "I want your very biggest chunk of laundry soap," he told Minda.

"The very biggest, eh?" she said, and slowly pulled out two pieces of cloth from under the counter. "Well now, does your mama like red or purple better?"

"Minda," said Kessy, "Mama doesn't want cloth. She wants the biggest soap!" He hopped from one foot to the other. "And hurry, please."

Minda spread out the red cloth. "To wrap around the soap," she said, and plunked down a great hunk. "As big and yellow as a bunch of ripe bananas, eh?"

She tied the cloth onto a sturdy stick. "To help your little shoulders carry the biggest soap," she said.

Kessy hoisted his bundle. "Hunh," he grunted. It was heavy, but Kessy just smiled and said, "Light as a handful of chicken feathers to me."

Now, he thought, I'll get home as speedy as Papa-chi's motorboat. And away he zoomed, until he came to the driftwood log.

There Amina sat howling—"Oww!"

Two of her fingers were bleeding. "I cut myself on my camera," she cried.

This time, Kessy stopped. He opened the red cloth. Then he cleaned Amina's cuts with seawater and the biggest soap.

"Thank you, Kessy," said Amina. And she placed her ginger
flower *maramar* on his head.

Kessy rewrapped the soap and rushed away—*rish-roosh*.

But as he ran toward Uncle Cho's house, an awful screeching
filled his ears. What *was* it? Was Uncle Cho in trouble?

SCREE! SCREE! Uncle Cho was sliding his new window up and down. "I can't smooth the edges enough to get them quiet," he said.

Kessy looked from the window to the packet on his shoulder. Once again, he unwrapped Mama's soap. "Will a piece of this help?" he asked.

"Let's find out," said Uncle Cho. With his pocketknife, he
sliced off a chunk and rubbed it along the edges of the window.
"Quiet as a ghost's shadow," said Uncle Cho, moving the
window open and shut. Then he handed Kessy the silver knife.
"Keep it till I see you tomorrow," he said.
"Thanks, Uncle," said Kessy. His fingers flew as he tied
the soap package back onto his stick.

By the time Kessy reached the mangroves, the sun was high in the sky. And standing in the middle of the path were two creatures, as stiff as tree trunks.

"Help! We're turning into mud statues!" hollered one. "The tide moved out before we could rinse off."

"We'd better get to the bathhouse and clean up before Mama sees us," cried the other. "Kessy, give us some soap!"

"Sorry, brothers, I can't stop," said Kessy, and hurried past them.

"But Kessy, you *have* to help us," Timus called after him.
"We'll get in trouble with Mama," cried Berto.
"Please," both brothers pleaded.

Kessy stopped. He turned and looked at his mud-caked brothers. Then
he unwrapped the soap and, quicker than Uncle Cho, carved off two pieces.
"For you, Itty-Bitty Mud Monsters," he said.

As Kessy rushed down the final stretch of path to the washing pool,
a cousin was about to begin the first story.

"Just in time," said Mama. "We need that soap."

"It's the *biggest* soap," Kessy announced as Mama unwrapped it.

"Well, it *was* the biggest soap," said Kessy.

"Mm-hmm," said Mama.

"Really," said Kessy. "It was so big that Minda had to lift it off the shelf with a stick—like prying a boulder from a mountain." Kessy showed Mama the stick.

"Minda told me to carry it on my strong-as-a-giant shoulders," said Kessy. "And I did. Until I, um . . . I heard a Fish-Spirit Girl calling from the beach—*Help! Help!*"

"A Fish-Spirit Girl?" said Mama as she rubbed the soap into a dirty shirt.

"Yes. She'd cut her fingers on the back of a Zigzag Sea Serpent," said Kessy. "Only some of the biggest soap mixed with seawater could help her."

Kessy tapped his head. "And she gave me this *maramar*, from a magical coral island."

"*Magical?*" wondered another cousin as she hung up a dress to dry.

"That's right," said Kessy. "But before I could ask about it, I heard Uncle Cho calling, 'Kessy, come quickly! There's a ghost screeching outside my new window.' "

"A *ghost*!" cried the cousins together.

"The kind of ghost," said Kessy, "that's scared away only by a chunk of the biggest yellow laundry soap cut with a silver knife."

"Oh-h," said the cousins, scrubbing away.

"I had the soap. Uncle Cho had the knife. That ghost left in a hurry," said Kessy. "And Uncle Cho gave me the knife."

"Ah-h," said the cousins.

"But then," said Kessy, "as I hurried along the path, two Giant Mud Monsters blocked my way. There was only one thing to do."

"And what was that?" said Mama. She hung a pair of pants on the line.

"*Swoosh, whoosh!*" cried Kessy.
"With two great pieces of the biggest soap, I scrubbed away till those monsters were as small as teensy hermit crabs."

"And till my soap was no bigger than a baby gecko," said Mama.

"But it was big enough," said a cousin. "Look. The wash lines are full."

Mama looked at the soap and then at Kessy. "You packed this little thing with enough suds and stories to get *all* the laundry done today," she said. "How did you do that, Mr. Big Storyteller?"

Kessy smiled as bright as an island sunrise. "I don't know," he said. "I guess it really *was* the biggest soap ever."

And then . . .

. . . the new big storyteller jumped right into the washing pool . . .

KER-SPLASH!